Ivy Makes a Craft

A Book about Measuring

BY CHARLY HALEY

Published by The Child's World®
1980 Lookout Drive • Mankato, MN 56003-1705
800-599-READ • www.childsworld.com

Photographs ©: Ruslan Guzov/Shutterstock Images, cover (foreground), 3, 4, 7, 16; Shutterstock Images, cover (background), 1, 11, 15 (background), 19; iStockphoto, 2, 6, 9, 10, 12 (middle), 15 (foreground), 23; Dragon Images/Shutterstock Images, 8; CE Photography/Shutterstock Images, 12 (top); Vitaly Zorkin/Shutterstock Images, 12 (bottom); Rob Marmion/Shutterstock Images, 20

Copyright © 2019 by The Child's World®
All rights reserved. No part of this book may be reproduced or utilized in any form or by any means without written permission from the publisher.

ISBN HARDCOVER: 9781503824928
ISBN PAPERBACK: 9781622434244
LCCN 2017964157

Printed in the United States of America
PA02387

About the Author

Charly Haley is a writer and children's book editor who lives in Minnesota. Aside from reading and writing, she enjoys music, yoga, and spending time with friends and family.

Today was a big day for Ivy. What did Ivy do today?

Ivy made a craft with her mom!

Ivy wanted her craft to be five **inches** long and four inches wide. She used a tool to help her measure.

She did not measure in **feet**. People measure how tall they are in feet.

She did not measure in **yards**. A football field is measured in yards.

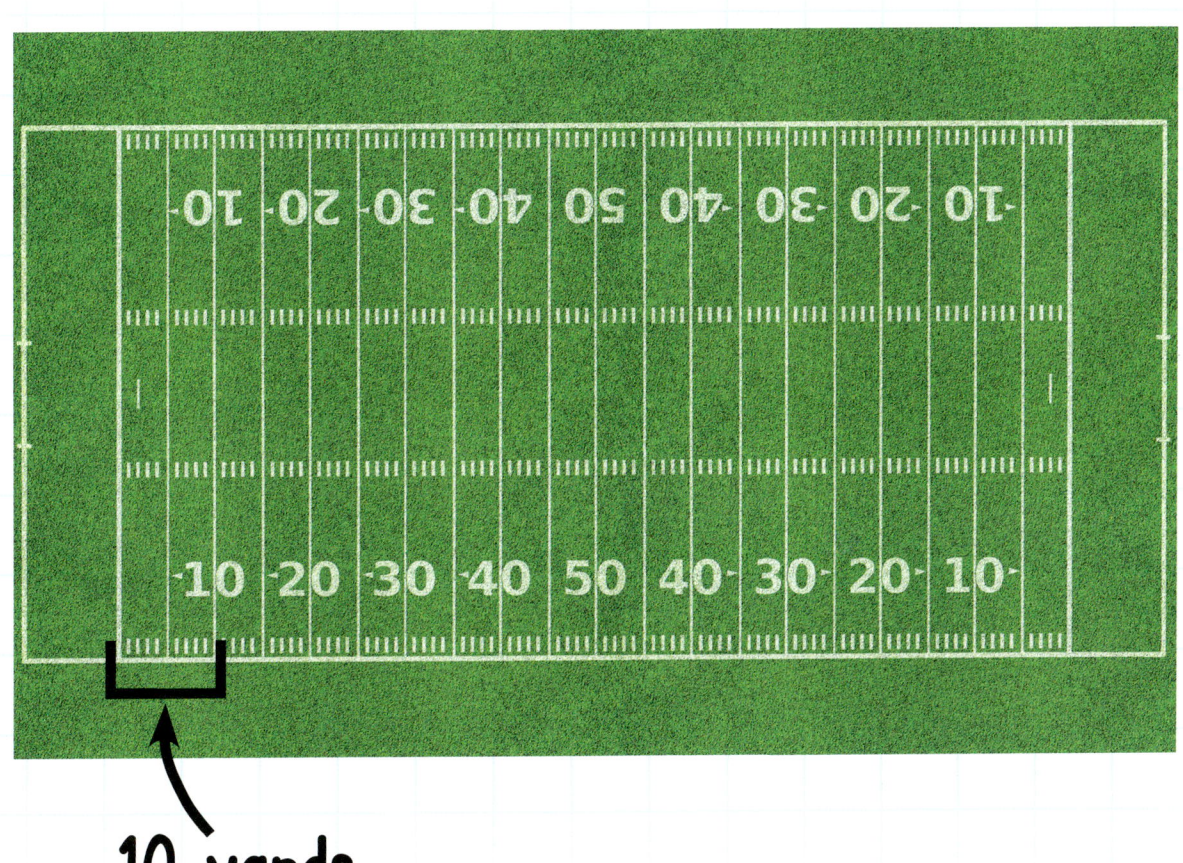

10 yards

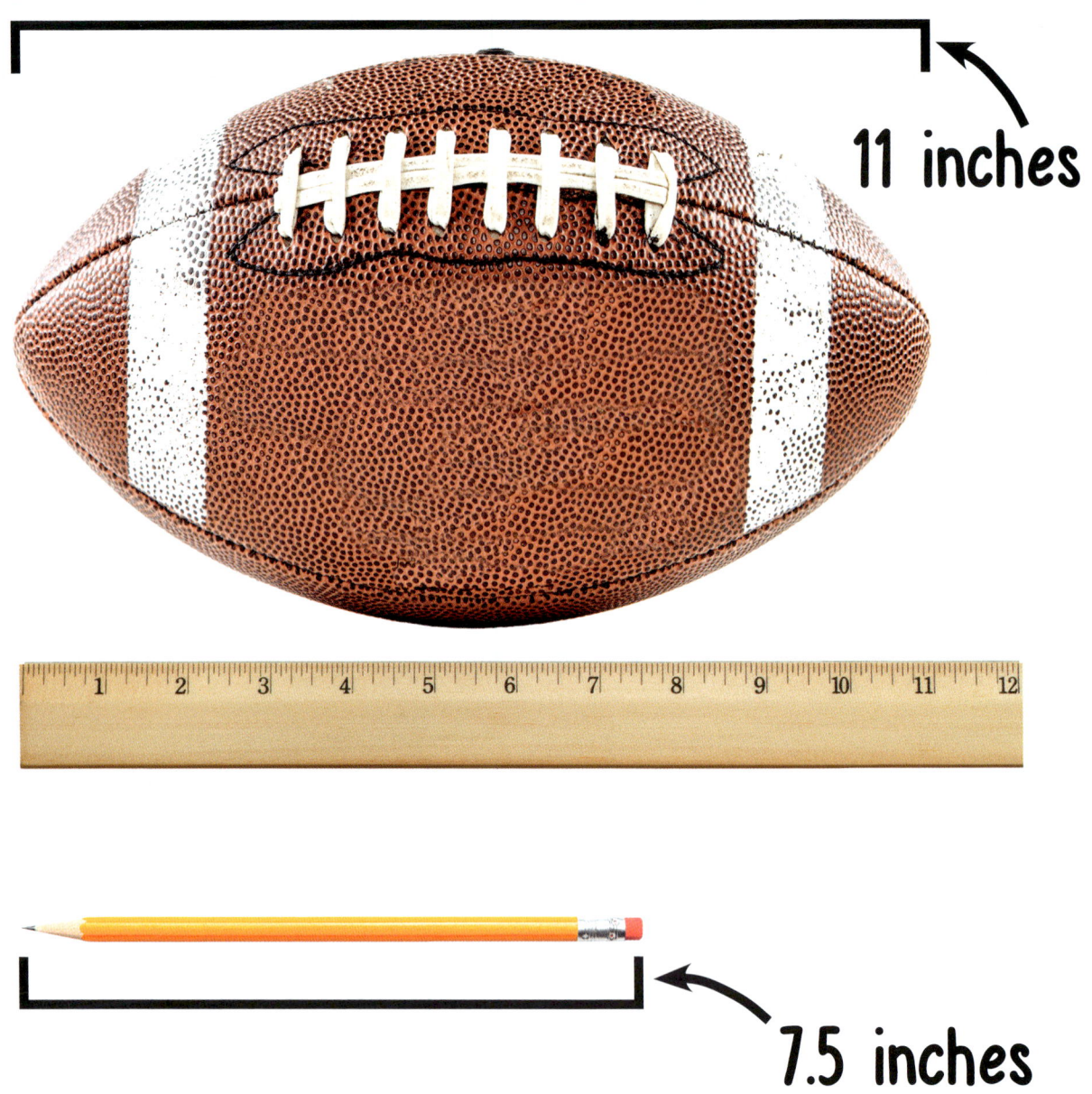

Ivy used a **ruler**. A ruler is one foot long. One foot is 12 inches. Perfect!

With her ruler, Ivy drew a shape that was five inches long and four inches wide.

Then Ivy cut out the paper and made her craft.

Ivy made a butterfly!

When do you measure things?

Words to Know

feet (FEET) People measure in feet to find out an object's length. There are three feet in one yard.

inches (INCH-ehz) People measure in inches when the object is small. There are 12 inches in one foot.

ruler (ROO-lur) A ruler is a tool for measuring. A ruler is normally one foot long.

yards (YARDS) People measure in yards when the object is large. Football fields have a length of 100 yards.

Extended Learning Activities

1. Why is it important to be able to measure things?

2. Length is just one example of a measurement. What are some other things that people measure?

3. If someone wanted to measure the length of a car, should they measure in inches, feet, or yards?

To Learn More

Books

Chatterjee, Anjana. *Measure Up*.
London, UK: QED Publishing, 2018.

Marton, Eleonora. *Bigger*.
London, UK: Cicada Books, 2017.

Vogel, Julia. *Measuring Volume*.
Mankato, MN: The Child's World, 2013.

Web Sites

Visit our Web site for links about measuring:

childsworld.com/links

Note to Parents, Teachers, and Librarians: We routinely verify our Web links to make sure they are safe and active sites. So encourage your readers to check them out!

ER
HAL

5/31/19